BALDWIN

SONNY'S BLUES AND OTHER STORIES

PENGUIN BOOKS

PENGUIN BOOKS

Published by the Penguin Group. Penguin Books Ltd, 27 Wrights Lane, London W8 5TZ, England. Penguin Books USA Inc., 375 Hudson Street, New York, New York 10014, USA. Penguin Books Australia Ltd, Ringwood, Victoria, Australia. Penguin Books Canada Ltd, 10 Alcorn Avenue, Toronto, Ontario, Canada M4V 3B2. Penguin Books (NZ) Ltd, 182–190 Wairau Road, Auckland 10, New Zealand · Penguin Books Ltd, Registered Offices: Harmondsworth, Middlesex, England · **These stories have been taken from *Going to Meet the Man* by James Baldwin, published by Penguin Books in 1991.** This edition published 1995 · Typeset by Datix International Limited, Bungay, Suffolk. Printed in England by Clays Ltd, St Ives plc ·
10 9 8 7 6 5 4 3 2 1

CONTENTS

Sonny's Blues

I read about it in the paper, in the subway, on my way to work. I read it, and I couldn't believe it, and I read it again. Then perhaps I just stared at it, at the newsprint spelling out his name, spelling out the story. I stared at it in the swinging lights of the subway car, and in the faces and bodies of the people, and in my own face, trapped in the darkness which roared outside.

It was not to be believed and I kept telling myself that as I walked from the subway station to the high school. And at the same time I couldn't doubt it. I was scared, scared for Sonny. He became real to me again. A great block of ice got settled in my belly and kept melting there slowly all day long, while I taught my classes algebra. It was a special kind of ice. It kept melting, sending trickles of ice water all up and down my veins, but it never got less. Sometimes it hardened and seemed to expand until I felt my guts were going to come spilling out or that I was going to choke or scream. This would always be at a moment when I was remembering some specific thing Sonny had once said or done.

When he was about as old as the boys in my classes his face had been bright and open, there was a lot of copper in it; and he'd had wonderfully direct brown eyes, and great gentleness and privacy. I wondered what he looked like now. He had been picked up, the evening before, in a raid on an apartment downtown, for peddling and using heroin.

I couldn't believe it: but what I mean by that is that I couldn't find any room for it anywhere inside me. I had kept it outside me for a long time. I hadn't wanted to know. I had had suspicions, but I didn't name them, I kept putting them away. I told myself that Sonny was wild, but he wasn't crazy. And he'd always been a good boy, he hadn't ever turned hard or evil or disrespectful, the way kids can, so quick, so quick, especially in Harlem. I didn't want to believe that I'd ever see my brother going down, coming to nothing, all that light in his face gone out, in the condition I'd already seen so many others. Yet it had happened and here I was, talking about algebra to a lot of boys who might, every one of them for all I knew, be popping off needles every time they went to the head. Maybe it did more for them than algebra could.

I was sure that the first time Sonny had ever had horse, he couldn't have been much older than these boys were now. These boys, now, were living as we'd been living then, they were growing up with a rush and their heads bumped abruptly against the low ceiling of their actual possibilities. They were filled with rage. All they really knew were two darknesses, the darkness of their lives, which was now closing in on them, and the darkness of the movies, which had blinded them to that other darkness, and in which they now, vindictively, dreamed, at once more together than they were at any other time, and more alone.

When the last bell rang, the last class ended, I let out my breath. It seemed I'd been holding it for all that time. My clothes were wet – I may have looked as though I'd been sitting in a steam bath, all dressed up, all afternoon. I sat alone in the classroom a long time. I listened to the boys outside, downstairs, shouting and cursing and laughing. Their laughter struck me for perhaps the first time. It was not the joyous laughter which – God knows why – one associates with children. It was mocking and insular, its intent was to denigrate. It was disenchanted, and in this, also, lay the authority of their curses. Perhaps I was listening to them because I was thinking about my brother and in them I heard my brother. And myself.

One boy was whistling a tune, at once very complicated and very simple, it seemed to be pouring out of him as though he were a bird, and it sounded very cool and moving through all that harsh, bright air, only just holding its own through all those other sounds.

I stood up and walked over to the window and looked down into the courtyard. It was the beginning of the spring and the sap was rising in the boys. A teacher passed through them every now and again, quickly, as though he or she couldn't wait to get out of that courtyard, to get those boys out of their sight and off their minds. I started collecting my stuff. I thought I'd better get home and talk to Isabel.

The courtyard was almost deserted by the time I got downstairs. I saw this boy standing in the shadow of a doorway, looking just like Sonny. I almost called his name. Then I saw that it wasn't Sonny, but somebody we used to know, a boy from around our block. He'd been Sonny's friend. He'd never been mine, having been too young for me, and, anyway, I'd never liked him. And now, even though he was a grown-up man, he still hung around that block, still spent hours on the street corners, was always high and raggy. I used to run into him from time to time and he'd often work around to asking me for a quarter or fifty cents. He always had some real good excuse, too, and I always gave it to him, I don't know why.

But now, abruptly, I hated him. I couldn't stand the way he looked at me, partly like a dog, partly like a cunning child. I wanted to ask him what the hell he was doing in the school courtyard.

He sort of shuffled over to me, and he said, 'I see you got the papers. So you already know about it.'

'You mean about Sonny? Yes, I already know about it. How come they didn't get you?'

He grinned. It made him repulsive and it also brought

to mind what he'd looked like as a kid. 'I wasn't there. I stay away from them people.'

'Good for you.' I offered him a cigarette and I watched him through the smoke. 'You come all the way down here just to tell me about Sonny?'

'That's right.' He was sort of shaking his head and his eyes looked strange, as though they were about to cross. The bright sun deadened his damp dark brown skin and it made his eyes look yellow and showed up the dirt in his conked hair. He smelled funky. I moved a little away from him and I said, 'Well, thanks. But I already know about it and I got to get home.'

'I'll walk you a little ways,' he said. We started walking. There were a couple of kids still loitering in the courtyard and one of them said good night to me and looked strangely at the boy beside me.

'What're you going to do?' he asked me. 'I mean, about Sonny?'

'Look. I haven't seen Sonny for over a year, I'm not sure I'm going to do anything. Anyway, what the hell *can* I do?'

'That's right,' he said quickly, 'ain't nothing you can do. Can't much help old Sonny no more, I guess.'

It was what I was thinking and so it seemed to me he had no right to say it.

'I'm surprised at Sonny, though,' he went on – he had a funny way of talking, he looked straight ahead as though he were talking to himself – ‘I thought Sonny was a smart boy, I thought he was too smart to get hung.’

‘I guess he thought so too,’ I said sharply, ‘and that’s how he got hung. And how about you? You’re pretty goddamn smart, I bet.’

Then he looked directly at me, just for a minute. ‘I ain’t smart,’ he said. ‘If I was smart, I’d have reached for a pistol a long time ago.’

‘Look. Don’t tell *me* your sad story, if it was up to me, I’d give you one.’ Then I felt guilty – guilty, probably, for never having supposed that the poor bastard *had* a story of his own, much less a sad one, and I asked, quickly, ‘What’s going to happen to him now?’

He didn’t answer this. He was off by himself some place. ‘Funny thing,’ he said, and from his tone we might have been discussing the quickest way to get to Brooklyn, ‘when I saw the papers this morning, the first thing I asked myself was if I had anything to do with it. I felt sort of responsible.’

I began to listen more carefully. The subway station was on the corner, just before us, and I stopped. He stopped, too. We were in front of a bar and he ducked slightly, peering in, but whoever he was looking for didn’t seem to be there. The juke box was blasting away with something black and bouncy and I half watched the barmaid as she danced her way from the juke box to her place behind the bar. And I watched her face as she laughingly responded to something someone said to her, still keeping time to the music. When she smiled one saw the little girl, one sensed the doomed, still-struggling woman beneath the battered face of the semi-whore.

'I never *give* Sonny nothing,' the boy said finally, 'but a long time ago I come to school high and Sonny asked me how it felt.' He paused, I couldn't bear to watch him, I watched the barmaid, and I listened to the music which seemed to be causing the pavement to shake. 'I told him it felt great.' The music stopped, the barmaid paused and watched the juke box until the music began again. 'It did.'

All this was carrying me some place I didn't want to go. I certainly didn't want to know how it felt. It filled everything, the people, the houses, the music, the dark, quicksilver barmaid, with menace; and this menace was their reality.

'What's going to happen to him now?' I asked again.

'They'll send him away some place and they'll try to cure him.' He shook his head. 'Maybe he'll even think he's kicked the habit. Then they'll let him loose' – he gestured, throwing his cigarette into the gutter. 'That's all.'

'What do you mean, that's *all*?'

But I knew what he meant.

'I *mean*, that's *all*.' He turned his head and looked at me, pulling down the corners of his mouth. 'Don't you know what I mean?' he asked, softly.

'How the hell *would* I know what you mean?' I almost whispered it, I don't know why.

'That's right,' he said to the air, 'how would *he* know what I mean?' He turned towards me again, patient and calm, and yet I somehow felt him shaking, shaking as though he were going to fall apart. I felt that ice in my guts again, the dread I'd felt all afternoon; and again I watched the barmaid, moving about the bar, washing glasses, and singing. 'Listen. They'll let him out and then it'll just start all over again. That's what I mean.'

'You mean – they'll let him out. And then he'll just start working his way back in again. You mean he'll never kick the habit. Is that what you mean?'

'That's right,' he said, cheerfully. '*You* see what I mean.'

'Tell me,' I said at last, 'why does he want to die? He must want to die, he's killing himself, why does he want to die?'

He looked at me in surprise. He licked his lips. 'He don't want to die. He wants to live. Don't nobody want to die, ever.'

Then I wanted to ask him – too many things. He could not have answered, or if he had, I could not have borne the answers. I started walking. 'Well, I guess it's none of my business.'

'It's going to be rough on old Sonny,' he said. We

 reached the subway station. 'This is your station?' he

asked. I nodded. I took one step down. 'Damn!' he said, suddenly. I looked up at him. He grinned again. 'Damn it if I didn't leave all my money home. You ain't got a dollar on you, have you? Just for a couple of days, is all.'

All at once something inside gave and threatened to come pouring out of me. I didn't hate him any more. I felt that in another moment I'd start crying like a child.

'Sure,' I said. 'Don't sweat.' I looked in my wallet and didn't have a dollar, I only had a five. 'Here,' I said. 'That hold you?'

He didn't look at it – he didn't want to look at it. A terrible, closed look came over his face, as though he were keeping the number on the bill a secret from him and me. 'Thanks,' he said, and now he was dying to see me go. 'Don't worry about Sonny. Maybe I'll write him or something.'

'Sure,' I said. 'You do that. So long.'

'Be seeing you,' he said. I went on down the steps.

And I didn't write Sonny or send him anything for a long time. When I finally did, it was just after my little girl died, he wrote me back a letter which made me feel like a bastard.

Here's what he said:

Dear brother,

You don't know how much I needed to hear from you. I

wanted to write you many a time but I dug how much I must have hurt you and so I didn't write. But now I feel like a man who's been trying to climb up out of some deep, real deep and funky hole and just saw the sun up there, outside. I got to get outside.

I can't tell you much about how I got here. I mean I don't know how to tell you. I guess I was afraid of something or I was trying to escape from something and you know I have never been very strong in the head (smile). I'm glad Mama and Daddy are dead and can't see what's happened to their son and I swear if I'd known what I was doing I would never have hurt you so, you and a lot of other fine people who were nice to me and who believed in me.

I don't want you to think it had anything to do with me being a musician. It's more than that. Or maybe less than that. I can't get anything straight in my head down here and I try not to think about what's going to happen to me when I get outside again. Sometime I think I'm going to flip and *never* get outside and sometime I think I'll come straight back. I tell you one thing, though, I'd rather blow my brains out than go through this again. But that's what they all say, so they tell me. If I tell you when I'm coming to New York and if you could meet me, I sure would appreciate it. Give my love to Isabel and the kids and I was sure sorry to hear about little Gracie. I wish I could be like Mama and say the Lord's will be done, but I don't know it seems to me that trouble is the one thing that never does get stopped and I don't know what good it does to blame it on the Lord. But maybe it does some good if you believe it.

Your brother,
Sonny

Then I kept in constant touch with him and I sent him whatever I could and I went to meet him when he came back to New York. When I saw him many things I thought I had forgotten came flooding back to me. This was because I had begun, finally, to wonder about Sonny, about the life that Sonny lived inside. This life, whatever it was, had made him older and thinner and it had deepened the distant stillness in which he had always moved. He looked very unlike my baby brother. Yet, when he smiled, when we shook hands, the baby brother I'd never known looked out from the depths of his private life, like an animal waiting to be coaxed into the light.

'How you been keeping?' he asked me.

'All right. And you?'

'Just fine.' He was smiling all over his face. 'It's good to see you again.'

'It's good to see you.'

The seven years' difference in our ages lay between us like a chasm: I wondered if these years would ever operate between us as a bridge. I was remembering, and it made it hard to catch my breath, that I had been there when he was born; and I had heard the first words he had ever spoken. When he started to walk, he walked from our mother straight to me. I caught him just before he fell when he took the first steps he ever took in this world.

'How's Isabel?'

'Just fine. She's dying to see you.'

'And the boys?'

'They're fine, too. They're anxious to see their uncle.'

'Oh, come on. You know they don't remember me.'

'Are you kidding? Of course they remember you.'

He grinned again. We got into a taxi. We had a lot to say to each other, far too much to know how to begin.

As the taxi began to move, I asked, 'You still want to go to India?'

He laughed. 'You still remember that. Hell, no. This place is Indian enough for me.'

'It used to belong to them,' I said.

And he laughed again. 'They damn sure knew what they were doing when they got rid of it.'

Years ago, when he was around fourteen, he'd been all hipped on the idea of going to India. He read books about people sitting on rocks, naked, in all kinds of weather, but mostly bad, naturally, and walking barefoot through hot coals and arriving at wisdom. I used to say that it sounded to me as though they were getting away from wisdom as fast as they could. I think he sort of looked down on me for that.

'Do you mind,' he asked, 'if we have the driver drive alongside the park? On the west side – I haven't seen the city in so long.'

'Of course not,' I said. I was afraid that I might sound

as though I were humoring him, but I hoped he wouldn't take it that way.

So we drove along, between the green of the park and the stony, lifeless elegance of hotels and apartment buildings, towards the vivid, killing streets of our childhood. These streets hadn't changed, though housing projects jutted up out of them now like rocks in the middle of a boiling sea. Most of the houses in which we had grown up had vanished, as had the stores from which we had stolen, the basements in which we had first tried sex, the rooftops from which we had hurled tin cans and bricks. But houses exactly like the houses of our past yet dominated the landscape, boys exactly like the boys we once had been found themselves smothering in these houses, came down into the streets for light and air and found themselves encircled by disaster. Some escaped the trap, most didn't. Those who got out always left something of themselves behind, as some animals amputate a leg and leave it in the trap. It might be said, perhaps, that I had escaped, after all, I was a school teacher; or that Sonny had, he hadn't lived in Harlem for years. Yet, as the cab moved uptown through streets which seemed, with a rush, to darken with dark people, and as I covertly studied Sonny's face, it came to me that what we both were seeking through our separate cab windows was that part of ourselves which had been left behind. It's always at the hour of trouble and confrontation that the missing member aches.

We hit 110th Street and started rolling up Lenox Avenue. And I'd known this avenue all my life, but it seemed to me again, as it had seemed on the day I'd first heard about Sonny's trouble, filled with a hidden menace which was its very breath of life.

'We almost there,' said Sonny.

'Almost.' We were both too nervous to say anything more.

We live in a housing project. It hasn't been up long. A few days after it was up it seemed uninhabitably new, now, of course, it's already rundown. It looks like a parody of the good, clean, faceless life – God knows the people who live in it do their best to make it a parody. The beat-looking grass lying around isn't enough to make their lives green, the hedges will never hold out the streets, and they know it. The big windows fool no one, they aren't big enough to make space out of no space. They don't bother with the windows, they watch the TV screen instead. The playground is most popular with the children who don't play at jacks, or skip rope, or roller skate, or swing, and they can be found in it after dark. We moved in partly because it's not too far from where I teach, and partly for the kids; but it's really just like the houses in which Sonny and I grew up. The same things happen, they'll have the same things to remember. The moment Sonny and I started into the house I had the feeling that I was simply bringing him back into the danger he had almost died trying to escape.

Sonny has never been talkative. So I don't know why I was sure he'd be dying to talk to me when supper was over the first night. Everything went fine, the oldest boy remembered him, and the youngest boy liked him, and Sonny had remembered to bring something for each of them; and Isabel, who is really much nicer than I am, more open and giving, had gone to a lot of trouble about dinner and was genuinely glad to see him. And she's always been able to tease Sonny in a way that I haven't. It was nice to see her face so vivid again and to hear her laugh and watch her make Sonny laugh. She wasn't, or, anyway, she didn't seem to be, at all uneasy or embarrassed. She chatted as though there were no subject which had to be avoided and she got Sonny past his first, faint stiffness. And thank God she was there, for I was filled with that icy dread again. Everything I did seemed awkward to me, and everything I said sounded freighted with hidden meaning. I was trying to remember everything I'd heard about dope addiction and I couldn't help watching Sonny for signs. I wasn't doing it out of malice. I was trying to find out something about my brother. I was dying to hear him tell me he was safe.

'Safe!' my father grunted, whenever Mama suggested trying to move to a neighborhood which might be safer for children. 'Safe, hell! Ain't no place safe for kids, nor nobody.'

He always went on like this, but he wasn't, ever, really

as bad as he sounded, not even on week-ends, when he got drunk. As a matter of fact, he was always on the lookout for 'something a little better', but he died before he found it. He died suddenly, during a drunken week-end in the middle of the war, when Sonny was fifteen. He and Sonny hadn't ever got on too well. And this was partly because Sonny was the apple of his father's eye. It was because he loved Sonny so much and was frightened for him, that he was always fighting with him. It doesn't do any good to fight with Sonny. Sonny just moves back, inside himself, where he can't be reached. But the principal reason that they never hit it off is that they were so much alike. Daddy was big and rough and loud-talking, just the opposite of Sonny, but they both had – that same privacy.

Mama tried to tell me something about this, just after Daddy died. I was home on leave from the army.

This was the last time I ever saw my mother alive. Just the same, this picture gets all mixed up in my mind with pictures I had of her when she was younger. The way I always see her is the way she used to be on a Sunday afternoon, say, when the old folks were talking after the big Sunday dinner. I always see her wearing pale blue. She'd be sitting on the sofa. And my father would be sitting in the easy chair, not far from her. And the living-room would be full of church folks and relatives. There they sit, in chairs all around the living-room, and the night is creeping up outside, but nobody knows it yet.

You can see the darkness growing against the window-panes and you hear the street noises every now and again, or maybe the jangling beat of a tambourine from one of the churches close by, but it's real quiet in the room. For a moment nobody's talking, but every face looks darkening, like the sky outside. And my mother rocks a little from the waist, and my father's eyes are closed. Everyone is looking at something a child can't see. For a minute they've forgotten the children. Maybe a kid is lying on the rug, half asleep. Maybe somebody's got a kid in his lap and is absent-mindedly stroking the kid's head. Maybe there's a kid, quiet and big-eyed, curled up in a big chair in the corner. The silence, the darkness coming, and the darkness in the faces frightens the child obscurely. He hopes that the hand which strokes his forehead will never stop – will never die. He hopes that there will never come a time when the old folks won't be sitting around the living-room, talking about where they've come from, and what they've seen, and what's happened to them and their kinfolk.

But something deep and watchful in the child knows that this is bound to end, is already ending. In a moment someone will get up and turn on the light. Then the old folks will remember the children and they won't talk any more that day. And when the light fills the room, the child is filled with darkness. He knows that every time this happens he's moved just a little closer to that darkness outside. The darkness outside is what the old folks have been talking about. It's what they've come from. It's what they endure. The child knows that they won't talk any more because if he knows too much about what's happened to *them*, he'll know too much too soon, about what's going to happen to *him*.

The last time I talked to my mother, I remember I was restless. I wanted to get out and see Isabel. We weren't married then and we had a lot to straighten out between us.

There Mama sat, in black, by the window. She was humming an old church song, *Lord, you brought me from a long ways off.* Sonny was out somewhere. Mama kept watching the streets.

'I don't know,' she said, 'if I'll ever see you again, after you go off from here. But I hope you'll remember the things I tried to teach you.'

'Don't talk like that,' I said, and smiled. 'You'll be here a long time yet.'

She smiled, too, but she said nothing. She was quiet for a long time. And I said, 'Mama, don't you worry about nothing. I'll be writing all the time, and you be getting the checks . . .'

'I want to talk to you about your brother,' she said, suddenly. 'If anything happens to me he ain't got to have nobody to look out for him.'

'Mama,' I said, 'ain't nothing going to happen to you *or*

Sonny. Sonny's all right. He's a good boy and he's got good sense.'

'It ain't a question of his being a good boy,' Mama said, 'nor of his having good sense. It ain't only the bad ones, nor yet the dumb ones that gets sucked under.' She stopped, looking at me. 'Your Daddy once had a brother,' she said, and she smiled in a way that made me feel she was in pain. 'You didn't never know that, did you?'

'No,' I said, 'I never knew that,' and I watched her face.

'Oh, yes,' she said, 'your Daddy had a brother.' She looked out of the window again. 'I know you never saw your Daddy cry. But *I* did – many a time, through all these years.'

I asked her, 'What happened to his brother? How come nobody's ever talked about him?'

This was the first time I ever saw my mother look old.

'His brother got killed,' she said, 'when he was just a little younger than you are now. I knew him. He was a fine boy. He was maybe a little full of the devil, but he didn't mean nobody no harm.'

Then she stopped and the room was silent, exactly as it had sometimes been on those Sunday afternoons. Mama kept looking out into the streets.

'He used to have a job in the mill,' she said, 'and, like all young folks, he just liked to perform on Saturday nights. Saturday nights, him and your father would drift around to different places, go to dances and things like that, or just sit around with people they knew and your father's brother would sing, he had a fine voice, and play along with himself on his guitar. Well, this particular Saturday night, him and your father was coming home from some place, and they were both a little drunk and there was a moon that night, it was bright like day. Your father's brother was feeling kind of good, and he was whistling to himself, and he had his guitar slung over his shoulder. They was coming down a hill and beneath them was a road that turned off from the highway. Well, your father's brother, being always kind of frisky, decided to run down this hill, and he did, with that guitar banging and clanging behind him, and he ran across the road, and he was making water behind a tree. And your father was sort of amused at him and he was still coming down the hill, kind of slow. Then he heard a car motor and that same minute his brother stepped from behind the tree, into the road, in the moonlight. And he started to cross the road. And your father started to run down the hill, he says he don't know why. This car was full of white men. They was all drunk, and when they seen your father's brother they let out a great whoop and holler and they aimed the car straight at him. They was having fun, they just wanted to scare him, the way they do sometimes, you know. But they was drunk. And I guess the boy, being drunk, too, and scared, kind of lost his head. By the time he jumped it was too late. Your father says he heard his brother scream when the car rolled over him, and he heard the wood of that guitar when it give, and he heard them strings go flying, and he heard them white men shouting, and the car kept on a-going and it ain't stopped till this day. And, time your father got down the hill, his brother weren't nothing but blood and pulp.'

Tears were gleaming on my mother's face. There wasn't anything I could say.

'He never mentioned it,' she said, 'because I never let him mention it before you children. Your Daddy was like a crazy man that night and for many a night thereafter. He says he never in his life seen anything as dark as that road after the lights of that car had gone away. Weren't nothing, weren't nobody on that road, just your Daddy and his brother and that busted guitar. Oh, yes. Your Daddy never did really get right again. Till the day he died he weren't sure but that every white man he saw was the man that killed his brother.'

She stopped and took out her handkerchief and dried her eyes and looked at me.

'I ain't telling you all this,' she said, 'to make you scared or bitter or to make you hate nobody. I'm telling you this because you got a brother. And the world ain't changed.'

I guess I didn't want to believe this. I guess she saw this in my face. She turned away from me, towards the window again, searching those streets.

'But I praise my Redeemer,' she said at last, 'that He called your Daddy home before me. I ain't saying it to throw no flowers at myself, but, I declare, it keeps me from feeling too cast down to know I helped your father get safely through this world. Your father always acted like he was the roughest, strongest man on earth. And everybody took him to be like that. But if he hadn't had *me* there – to see his tears!'

She was crying again. Still, I couldn't move. I said, 'Lord, Lord, Mama, I didn't know it was like that.'

'Oh, honey,' she said, 'there's a lot that you don't know. But you are going to find it out.' She stood up from the window and came over to me. 'You got to hold on to your brother,' she said, 'and don't let him fall, no matter what it looks like is happening to him and no matter how evil you gets with him. You going to be evil with him many a time. But don't you forget what I told you, you hear?'

'I won't forget,' I said. 'Don't you worry, I won't forget. I won't let nothing happen to Sonny.'

My mother smiled as though she were amused at something she saw in my face. Then, 'You may not be able to stop nothing from happening. But you got to let him know you's *there*.'

Two days later I was married, and then I was gone. And I had a lot of things on my mind and I pretty well forgot my promise to Mama until I got shipped home on a special furlough for her funeral.

And, after the funeral, with just Sonny and me alone in the empty kitchen, I tried to find out something about him.

'What do you want to do?' I asked him.

'I'm going to be a musician,' he said.

For he had graduated, in the time I had been away, from dancing to the juke box to finding out who was playing what, and what they were doing with it, and he had bought himself a set of drums.

'You mean, you want to be a drummer?' I somehow had the feeling that being a drummer might be all right for other people but not for my brother Sonny.

'I don't think,' he said, looking at me very gravely, 'that I'll ever be a good drummer. But I think I can play a piano.'

I frowned. I'd never played the role of the older brother quite so seriously before, had scarcely ever, in fact, *asked* Sonny a damn thing. I sensed myself in the presence of something I didn't really know how to handle, didn't understand. So I made my frown a little deeper as I asked: 'What kind of musician do you want to be?'

He grinned. 'How many kinds do you think there are?'

'Be *serious*,' I said.

He laughed, throwing his head back, and then looked at me. 'I *am* serious.'

'Well, then, for Christ's sake, stop kidding around and answer a serious question. I mean, do you want to be a concert pianist, you want to play classical music and all that, or – or what?' Long before I finished he was laughing again. 'For Christ's *sake*, Sonny!'

He sobered, but with difficulty. 'I'm sorry. But you sound so – *scared*!' and he was off again.

'Well, you may think it's funny now, baby, but it's not going to be so funny when you have to make your living at it, let me tell you *that*.' I was furious because I knew he was laughing at me and I didn't know why.

'No,' he said, very sober now, and afraid, perhaps, that he'd hurt me, 'I don't want to be a classical pianist. That isn't what interests me. I mean' – he paused, looking hard at me, as though his eyes would help me to understand, and then gestured helplessly, as though perhaps his hand would help – 'I mean, I'll have a lot of studying to do, and I'll have to study *everything*, but, I mean, I want to play *with* – jazz musicians.' He stopped. 'I want to play jazz,' he said.

Well, the word had never before sounded as heavy, as real, as it sounded that afternoon in Sonny's mouth. I just looked at him and I was probably frowning a real frown by this time. I simply couldn't see why on earth he'd want to spend his time hanging around night-clubs, clowning around on bandstands, while people pushed each other around on a dance floor. It seemed – beneath him, somehow. I had never thought about it before, had never been forced to, but I suppose I had always put jazz musicians in a class with what Daddy called 'good-time people'.

'Are you *serious*?'

'Hell, *yes*, I'm serious.'

He looked more helpless than ever, and annoyed, and deeply hurt.

I suggested, helpfully: 'You mean – like Louis Armstrong?'

His face closed as though I'd struck him. 'No. I'm not talking about none of that old-time, down-home crap.'

'Well, look, Sonny, I'm sorry, don't get mad. I just don't altogether get it, that's all. Name somebody – you know, a jazz musician you admire.'

'Bird.'

'Who?'

'Bird! Charlie Parker! Don't they teach you nothing in the goddamn army?'

I lit a cigarette. I was surprised and then a little amused to discover that I was trembling. 'I've been out of touch,' I said. 'You'll have to be patient with me. Now. Who's this Parker character?'

'He's just one of the greatest jazz musicians alive,' said Sonny, sullenly, his hands in his pockets, his back to me. 'Maybe *the* greatest,' he added, bitterly, 'that's probably why *you* never heard of him.'

'All right,' I said, 'I'm ignorant. I'm sorry. I'll go out and buy all the cat's records right away, all right?'

'It don't,' said Sonny, with dignity, 'make any difference to me. I don't care what you listen to. Don't do me no favors.'

I was beginning to realize that I'd never seen him so upset before. With another part of my mind I was thinking that this would probably turn out to be one of those things kids go through and that I shouldn't make it seem important by pushing it too hard. Still, I didn't think it would do any harm to ask: 'Doesn't all this take a lot of time? Can you make a living at it?'

He turned back to me and half leaned, half sat, on the kitchen table. 'Everything takes time,' he said, 'and – well, yes, sure, I can make a living at it. But what I don't seem to be able to make you understand is that it's the only thing I want to do.'

'Well, Sonny,' I said, gently, 'you know people can't always do exactly what they *want* to do –'

'*No*, I don't know that,' said Sonny, surprising me. 'I think people *ought* to do what they want to do, what else are they alive for?'

'You getting to be a big boy,' I said desperately, 'it's time you started thinking about your future.'

'I'm thinking about my future,' said Sonny, grimly. 'I think about it all the time.'

I gave up. I decided, if he didn't change his mind, that we could always talk about it later. 'In the meantime,' I said, 'you got to finish school.' We had already decided that he'd have to move in with Isabel and her folks. I knew this wasn't the ideal arrangement because Isabel's

 folks are inclined to be dicey and they hadn't especially

wanted Isabel to marry me. But I didn't know what else to do. 'And we have to get you fixed up at Isabel's.'

There was a long silence. He moved from the kitchen table to the window. 'That's a terrible idea. You know it yourself.'

'Do you have a *better* idea?'

He just walked up and down the kitchen for a minute. He was as tall as I was. He had started to shave. I suddenly had the feeling that I didn't know him at all.

He stopped at the kitchen table and picked up my cigarettes. Looking at me with a kind of mocking, amused defiance, he put one between his lips. 'You mind?'

'You smoking already?'

He lit the cigarette and nodded, watching me through the smoke. 'I just wanted to see if I'd have the courage to smoke in front of you.' He grinned and blew a great cloud of smoke to the ceiling. 'It was easy.' He looked at my face. 'Come on, now. I bet you was smoking at my age, tell the truth.'

I didn't say anything but the truth was on my face, and he laughed. But now there was something very strained in his laugh. 'Sure. And I bet that ain't all you was doing.'

He was frightening me a little. 'Cut the crap,' I said. 'We already decided that you was going to go and live at Isabel's. Now what's got into you all of a sudden?'

'*You* decided it,' he pointed out. '*I* didn't decide nothing.' He stopped in front of me, leaning against the stove, arms loosely folded. 'Look, brother. I don't want to stay in Harlem no more, I really don't.' He was very earnest. He looked at me, then over towards the kitchen window. There was something in his eyes I'd never seen before, some thoughtfulness, some worry all his own. He rubbed the muscle of one arm. 'It's time I was getting out of here.'

'Where do you want to *go*, Sonny?'

'I want to join the army. Or the navy, I don't care. If I say I'm old enough, they'll believe me.'

Then I got mad. It was because I was so scared. 'You must be crazy. You goddamn fool, what the hell do you want to go and join the *army* for?'

'I just told you. To get out of Harlem.'

'Sonny, you haven't even finished *school*. And if you really want to be a musician, how do you expect to study if you're in the *army*?'

He looked at me, trapped, and in anguish. 'There's ways. I might be able to work out some kind of deal. Anyway, I'll have the GI Bill when I come out.'

'*If* you come out.' We stared at each other. 'Sonny, please. Be reasonable. I know the set-up is far from perfect. But we got to do the best we can.'

'I ain't learning nothing in school,' he said. 'Even when I go.' He turned away from me and opened the window and threw his cigarette out into the narrow alley. I watched his back. 'At least, I ain't learning nothing you'd want me to learn.' He slammed the window so hard I thought the glass would fly out, and turned back to me. 'And I'm sick of the stink of these garbage cans!'

'Sonny,' I said, 'I know how you feel. But if you don't finish school now, you're going to be sorry later that you didn't.' I grabbed him by the shoulders. 'And you only got another year. It ain't so bad. And I'll come back and I swear I'll help you do *whatever* you want to do. Just try to put up with it till I come back. Will you please do that? For me?'

He didn't answer and he wouldn't look at me.

'Sonny. You hear me?'

He pulled away. 'I hear you. But you never hear anything *I* say.'

I didn't know what to say to that. He looked out of the window and then back at me. 'OK,' he said, and sighed. 'I'll try.'

Then I said, trying to cheer him up a little, 'They got a piano at Isabel's. You can practice on it.'

And as a matter of fact, it did cheer him up for a minute. 'That's right,' he said to himself. 'I forgot that.' His face relaxed a little. But the worry, the thoughtfulness, played on it still, the way shadows play on a face which is staring into the fire.

But I thought I'd never hear the end of that piano. At first, Isabel would write me, saying how nice it was that

Sonny was so serious about his music and how, as soon as he came in from school, or wherever he had been when he was supposed to be at school, he went straight to that piano and stayed there until suppertime. And, after supper, he went back to that piano and stayed there until everybody went to bed. He was at the piano all day Saturday and all day Sunday. Then he bought a record player and started playing records. He'd play one record over and over again, all day long sometimes, and he'd improvise along with it on the piano. Or he'd play one section of the record, one chord, one change, one progression, then he'd do it on the piano. Then back to the record. Then back to the piano.

Well, I really don't know how they stood it. Isabel finally confessed that it wasn't like living with a person at all, it was like living with sound. And the sound didn't make any sense to her, didn't make any sense to any of them – naturally. They began, in a way, to be afflicted by this presence that was living in their home. It was as though Sonny were some sort of god, or monster. He moved in an atmosphere which wasn't like theirs at all. They fed him and he ate, he washed himself, he walked in and out of their door; he certainly wasn't nasty or unpleasant or rude, Sonny isn't any of those things; but it was as though he were all wrapped up in some cloud, some fire, some vision all his own; and there wasn't any way to reach him.

At the same time, he wasn't really a man yet, he was still a child, and they had to watch out for him in all kinds of ways. They certainly couldn't throw him out. Neither did they dare to make a great scene about that piano because even they dimly sensed, as I sensed, from so many thousands of miles away, that Sonny was at that piano playing for his life.

But he hadn't been going to school. One day a letter came from the school board and Isabel's mother got it – there had, apparently, been other letters but Sonny had torn them up. This day, when Sonny came in, Isabel's mother showed him the letter and asked where he'd been spending his time. And she finally got it out of him that he'd been down in Greenwich Village, with musicians and other characters, in a white girl's apartment. And this scared her and she started to scream at him and what came up, once she began – though she denies it to this day – was what sacrifices they were making to give Sonny a decent home and how little he appreciated it.

Sonny didn't play the piano that day. By evening, Isabel's mother had calmed down but then there was the old man to deal with, and Isabel herself. Isabel says she did her best to be calm but she broke down and started crying. She says she just watched Sonny's face. She could tell, by watching him, what was happening with him. And what was happening was that they penetrated his cloud, they had reached him. Even if their fingers had been a thousand times more gentle than human fingers ever are, he could hardly help feeling that they had stripped him naked and were spitting on that nakedness. For he also had to see that his presence, that music, which was life or death to him, had been torture for them and that they had endured it, not at all for his sake, but only for mine. And Sonny couldn't take that. He can take it a little better today than he could then but he's still not very good at it and, frankly, I don't know anybody who is.

The silence of the next few days must have been louder than the sound of all the music ever played since time began. One morning, before she went to work, Isabel was in his room for something and she suddenly realized that all of his records were gone. And she knew for certain that he was gone. And he was. He went as far as the navy would carry him. He finally sent me a postcard from some place in Greece and that was the first I knew that Sonny was still alive. I didn't see him any more until we were both back in New York and the war had long been over.

He was a man by then, of course, but I wasn't willing to see it. He came by the house from time to time, but we fought almost every time we met. I didn't like the way he carried himself, loose and dreamlike all the time, and I didn't like his friends, and his music seemed to be merely an excuse for the life he led. It sounded just that weird and disordered.

 Then we had a fight, a pretty awful fight, and I didn't

see him for months. By and by I looked him up, where he was living, in a furnished room in the Village, and I tried to make it up. But there were lots of other people in the room and Sonny just lay on his bed, and he wouldn't come downstairs with me, and he treated these other people as though they were his family and I weren't. So I got mad and then he got mad, and then I told him that he might just as well be dead as live the way he was living. Then he stood up and he told me not to worry about him any more in life, that he *was* dead as far as I was concerned. Then he pushed me to the door and the other people looked on as though nothing were happening, and he slammed the door behind me. I stood in the hallway, staring at the door. I heard somebody laugh in the room and then the tears came to my eyes. I started down the steps, whistling to keep from crying, I kept whistling to myself, *You going to need me baby one of these cold, rainy days.*

I read about Sonny's trouble in the spring. Little Grace died in the fall. She was a beautiful little girl. But she only lived a little over two years. She died of polio and she suffered. She had a slight fever for a couple of days, but it didn't seem like anything and we just kept her in bed. And we would certainly have called the doctor, but the fever dropped, she seemed to be all right. So we thought it had just been a cold. Then, one day, she was up, playing, Isabel was in the kitchen fixing lunch for the two boys when they'd come in from school, and she heard Grace fall down in the living-room. When you have a lot of children you don't always start running when one of them falls, unless they start screaming or something. And, this time, Grace was quiet. Yet, Isabel says that when she heard that *thump* and then that silence, something happened in her to make her afraid. And she ran to the living-room and there was little Grace on the floor, all twisted up, and the reason she hadn't screamed was that she couldn't get her breath. And when she did scream, it was the worst sound, Isabel says, that she'd ever heard in all her life, and she still hears it sometimes in her dreams. Isabel will sometimes wake me up with a low, moaning, strangled sound and I have to be quick to awaken her and hold her to me and where Isabel is weeping against me seems a mortal wound.

I think I may have written Sonny the very day that little Grace was buried. I was sitting in the living-room in the dark, by myself, and I suddenly thought of Sonny. My trouble made his real.

One Saturday afternoon, when Sonny had been living with us, or, anyway, been in our house, for nearly two weeks, I found myself wandering aimlessly about the living-room, drinking from a can of beer, and trying to work up the courage to search Sonny's room. He was out, he was usually out whenever I was home, and Isabel had taken the children to see their grandparents. Suddenly I was standing still in front of the living-room window, watching Seventh Avenue. The idea of searching Sonny's room made me still. I scarcely dared to admit to myself what I'd be searching for. I didn't know what I'd do if I found it. Or if I didn't.

On the sidewalk across from me, near the entrance to a barbecue joint, some people were holding an old-fashioned revival meeting. The barbecue cook, wearing a dirty white apron, his conked hair reddish and metallic in the pale sun, and a cigarette between his lips, stood in the doorway, watching them. Kids and older people paused in their errands and stood there, along with some older men and a couple of very tough-looking women who watched everything that happened on the avenue, as though they owned it, or were maybe owned by it. Well, they were watching this, too. The revival was being carried on by three sisters in black, and a brother. All they had were their voices and their Bibles and a tambourine. The brother was testifying and while he testified two of the sisters stood together, seeming to say, amen, and the third sister walked around with the tambourine outstretched and a couple of people dropped coins into it. Then the brother's testimony ended and the sister who had been taking up the collection dumped the coins into her palm and transferred them to the pocket of her long black robe. Then she raised both hands, striking the tambourine against the air, and then against one hand, and she started to sing. And the two other sisters and the brother joined in.

It was strange, suddenly, to watch, though I had been seeing these street meetings all my life. So, of course, had everybody else down there. Yet, they paused and watched and listened and I stood still at the window. ''*Tis the old ship of Zion*,' they sang, and the sister with the tambourine kept a steady, jangling beat, '*it has rescued many a thousand!*' Not a soul under the sound of their voices was hearing this song for the first time, not one of them had been rescued. Nor had they seen much in the way of rescue work being done around them. Neither did they especially believe in the holiness of the three sisters and the brother, they knew too much about them, knew where they lived, and how. The woman with the tambourine, whose voice dominated the air, whose face was bright with joy, was divided by very little from the woman who stood watching her, a cigarette between her heavy, chapped lips, her hair a cuckoo's nest, her face scarred and swollen from many beatings, and her black eyes glittering like coal. Perhaps they both knew this, which was why, when, as rarely, they addressed each other, they addressed each other as Sister. As the singing filled the air the watching, listening faces underwent a change, the eyes focusing on something within; the music seemed to soothe a poison out of them; and time seemed, nearly, to fall away from the sullen, belligerent, battered faces, as though they were fleeing back to their first condition, while dreaming of their last. The barbecue cook half shook his head and smiled, and dropped his cigarette and disappeared into his joint. A man fumbled in his pockets for change and stood holding it in his hand impatiently, as though he had just remembered a pressing appointment further up the avenue. He looked furious. Then I saw Sonny, standing on the edge of the crowd. He was carrying a wide, flat notebook with a green cover, and it made him look, from where I was standing, almost like a schoolboy. The coppery sun brought out the copper in his skin, he was very faintly smiling, standing very still. Then the singing stopped, the tambourine turned into a collection plate again. The furious man dropped in his coins and vanished, so did a couple of the women, and Sonny dropped some change in the plate, looking directly at the women with a little smile. He started across the avenue, towards the house. He has a slow, loping walk, something like the way Harlem hipsters walk, only he's imposed on this his own half-beat. I had never really noticed it before.

I stayed at the window, both relieved and apprehensive. As Sonny disappeared from my sight, they began singing again. And they were still singing when his key turned in the lock.

'Hey,' he said.

'Hey, yourself. You want some beer?'

'No. Well, maybe.' But he came up to the window and stood beside me, looking out. 'What a warm voice,' he said.

They were singing, '*If I could only hear my mother pray again!*'

'Yes,' I said, 'and she can sure beat that tambourine.'

'But what a terrible song,' he said, and laughed. He dropped his notebook on the sofa and disappeared into the kitchen. 'Where's Isabel and the kids?'

'I think they went to see their grandparents. You hungry?'

'No.' He came back into the living-room with his can of beer. 'You want to come some place with me tonight?'

I sensed, I don't know how, that I couldn't possibly say no. 'Sure. Where?'

He sat down on the sofa and picked up his notebook and started leafing through it. 'I'm going to sit in with some fellows in a joint in the Village.'

'You mean, you're going to play, tonight?'

'That's right.' He took a swallow of his beer and moved back to the window. He gave me a sidelong look. 'If you can stand it.'

'I'll try,' I said.

He smiled to himself and we both watched as the meeting across the way broke up. The three sisters and the brother, heads bowed, were singing, '*God be with you till we meet again.*' The faces around them were very quiet. Then the song ended. The small crowd dispersed.

We watched the three women and the lone man walk slowly up the avenue.

'When she was singing before,' said Sonny, abruptly, 'her voice reminded me for a minute of what heroin feels like sometimes – when it's in your veins. It makes you feel sort of warm and cool at the same time. And distant. And – and sure.' He sipped his beer, very deliberately not looking at me. I watched his face. 'It makes you feel – in control. Sometimes you've got to have that feeling.'

'Do you?' I sat down slowly in the easy chair.

'Sometimes.' He went to the sofa and picked up his notebook again. 'Some people do.'

'In order,' I asked, 'to play?' And my voice was very ugly, full of contempt and anger.

'Well' – he looked at me with great, troubled eyes, as though, in fact, he hoped his eyes would tell me things he could never otherwise say – 'they *think* so. And *if* they think so –!'

'And what do *you* think?' I asked.

He sat on the sofa and put his can of beer on the floor. 'I don't know,' he said, and I couldn't be sure if he were answering my question or pursuing his thoughts. His face didn't tell me. 'It's not so much to *play*. It's to *stand* it, to be able to make it at all. On any level.' He frowned and smiled: 'In order to keep from shaking to pieces.'

'But these friends of yours,' I said, 'they seem to shake themselves to pieces pretty goddamn fast.'

'Maybe.' He played with the notebook. And something told me that I should curb my tongue, that Sonny was doing his best to talk, that I should listen. 'But of course you only know the ones that've gone to pieces. Some don't – or at least they haven't *yet* and that's just about all *any* of us can say.' He paused. 'And then there are some who just live, really, in hell, and they know it and they see what's happening and they go right on. I don't know.' He sighed, dropped the notebook, folded his arms. 'Some guys, you can tell from the way they play, they on something *all* the time. And you can see that, well, it makes something real for them. But of course,' he picked up his beer from the floor and sipped it and put the can down again, 'they *want* to, too, you've got to see that. Even some of them that say they don't – *some*, not all.'

'And what about you?' I asked – I couldn't help it. 'What about you? Do *you* want to?'

He stood up and walked to the window and remained silent for a long time. Then he sighed. 'Me,' he said. Then: 'While I was downstairs before, on my way here, listening to that woman sing, it struck me all of a sudden how much suffering she must have had to go through – to sing like that. It's *repulsive* to think you have to suffer that much.'

I said: 'But there's no way not to suffer – is there, Sonny?'

 'I believe not,' he said and smiled, 'but that's never

stopped anyone from trying.' He looked at me. 'Has it?' I realized, with this mocking look, that there stood between us, for ever, beyond the power of time or forgiveness, the fact that I had held silence – so long! – when he had needed human speech to help him. He turned back to the window. 'No, there's no way not to suffer. But you try all kinds of ways to keep from drowning in it, to keep on top of it, and to make it seem – well, like *you*. Like you did something, all right, and now you're suffering for it. You know?' I said nothing. 'Well you know,' he said, impatiently, 'why *do* people suffer? Maybe it's better to do something to give it a reason, *any* reason.'

'But we just agreed,' I said, 'that there's no way not to suffer. Isn't it better, then, just to – take it?'

'But nobody just takes it,' Sonny cried, 'that's what I'm telling you! *Everybody* tries not to. You're just hung up on the *way* some people try – it's not *your* way!'

The hair on my face began to itch, my face felt wet. 'That's not true,' I said, 'that's not true. I don't give a damn what other people do, I don't even care how they suffer. I just care how *you* suffer.' And he looked at me. 'Please believe me,' I said, 'I don't want to see you – die – trying not to suffer.'

'I won't,' he said, flatly, 'die trying not to suffer. At least, not any faster than anybody else.'

'But there's no need,' I said, trying to laugh, 'is there? in killing yourself.'

I wanted to say more, but I couldn't. I wanted to talk about will power and how life could be – well, beautiful. I wanted to say that it was all within; but was it? or, rather, wasn't that exactly the trouble? And I wanted to promise that I would never fail him again. But it would all have sounded – empty words and lies.

So I made the promise to myself and prayed that I would keep it.

'It's terrible sometimes, inside,' he said, 'that's what's the trouble. You walk these streets, black and funky and cold, and there's not really a living ass to talk to, and there's nothing shaking, and there's no way of getting it out – that storm inside. You can't talk it and you can't make love with it, and when you finally try to get with it and play it, you realize *nobody's* listening. So *you've* got to listen. You got to find a way to listen.'

And then he walked away from the window and sat on the sofa again, as though all the wind had suddenly been knocked out of him. 'Sometimes you'll do *anything* to play, even cut your mother's throat.' He laughed and looked at me. 'Or your brother's.' Then he sobered. 'Or your own.' Then: 'Don't worry. I'm all right now and I think I'll *be* all right. But I can't forget – where I've been. I don't mean just the physical place I've been, I mean where I've *been*. And *what* I've been.'

'What have you been, Sonny?' I asked.

 He smiled – but sat sideways on the sofa, his elbow

resting on the back, his fingers playing with his mouth and chin, not looking at me. 'I've been something I didn't recognize, didn't know I could be. Didn't know anybody could be.' He stopped, looking inward, looking helplessly young, looking old. 'I'm not talking about it now because I feel *guilty* or anything like that – maybe it would be better if I did, I don't know. Anyway, I can't really talk about it. Not to you, not to anybody,' and now he turned and faced me. 'Sometimes, you know, and it was actually when I was most *out* of the world, I felt that I was in it, that I was *with* it, really, and I could play or I didn't really have to *play*, it just came out of me, it was there. And I don't know how I played, thinking about it now, but I know I did awful things, those times, sometimes, to people. Or it wasn't that I *did* anything to them – it was that they weren't real.' He picked up the beer can; it was empty; he rolled it between his palms: 'And other times – well, I needed a fix, I needed to find a place to lean, I needed to clear a space to *listen* – and I couldn't find it, and I – went crazy, I did terrible things to *me*, I was terrible *for* me.' He began pressing the beer can between his hands, I watched the metal begin to give. It glittered, as he played with it, like a knife, and I was afraid he would cut himself, but I said nothing. 'Oh well. I can never tell you, I was all by myself at the bottom of something, stinking and sweating and crying and shaking, and I smelled it, you know? *my* stink, and I thought I'd die if I couldn't get away from it and yet, all the same, I knew that everything I was doing was just locking me in with it. And I didn't know,' he paused, still flattening the beer can, 'I didn't know, I still *don't* know, something kept telling me that maybe it was good to smell your own stink, but I didn't think that *that* was what I'd been trying to do – and – who can stand it?' and he abruptly dropped the ruined beer can, looking at me with a small, still smile, and then rose, walking to the window as though it were the lodestone rock. I watched his face, he watched the avenue. 'I couldn't tell you when Mama died – but the reason I wanted to leave Harlem so bad was to get away from drugs. And then, when I ran away, that's what I was running from – really. When I came back, nothing had changed, *I* hadn't changed, I was just – older.' And he stopped, drumming with his fingers on the window-pane. The sun had vanished, soon darkness would fall. I watched his face. 'It can come again,' he said, almost as though speaking to himself. Then he turned to me. 'It can come again,' he repeated. 'I just want you to know that.'

'All right,' I said, at last. 'So it can come again, all right.'

He smiled, but the smile was sorrowful. 'I had to try to tell you,' he said.

'Yes,' I said. 'I understand that.'

'You're my brother,' he said, looking straight at me, and not smiling at all.

'Yes,' I repeated, 'yes. I understand that.'

He turned back to the window, looking out. 'All that hatred down there,' he said, 'all that hatred and misery and love. It's a wonder it doesn't blow the avenue apart.'

We went to the only night-club on a short, dark street, downtown. We squeezed through the narrow, chattering, jam-packed bar to the entrance of the big room, where the bandstand was. And we stood there for a moment, for the lights were very dim in this room and we couldn't see. Then, 'Hello, boy,' said a voice and an enormous black man, much older than Sonny or myself, erupted out of all that atmospheric lighting and put an arm around Sonny's shoulder. 'I been sitting right here,' he said, 'waiting for you.'

He had a big voice, too, and heads in the darkness turned towards us.

Sonny grinned and pulled a little away, and said, 'Creole, this is my brother. I told you about him.'

Creole shook my hand. 'I'm glad to meet you, son,' he said, and it was clear that he was glad to meet me *there*, for Sonny's sake. And he smiled, 'You got a real musician in *your* family,' and he took his arm from Sonny's shoulder and slapped him, lightly, affectionately, with the back of his hand.

'Well. Now I've heard it all,' said a voice behind us. This was another musician, and a friend of Sonny's, a coal-black, cheerful-looking man, built close to the ground. He immediately began confiding to me, at the top of his lungs, the most terrible things about Sonny, his teeth gleaming like a lighthouse and his laugh coming up out of him like the beginning of an earthquake. And it turned out that everyone at the bar knew Sonny, or almost everyone; some were musicians, working there, or near by, or not working, some were simply hangers-on, and some were there to hear Sonny play. I was introduced to all of them and they were all very polite to me. Yet, it was clear that, for them, I was only Sonny's brother. Here, I was in Sonny's world. Or, rather: his kingdom. Here, it was not even a question that his veins bore royal blood.

They were going to play soon and Creole installed me, by myself, at a table in a dark corner. Then I watched them, Creole, and the little black man, and Sonny, and the others, while they horsed around, standing just below the bandstand. The light from the bandstand spilled just a little short of them and, watching them laughing and gesturing and moving about, I had the feeling that they, nevertheless, were being most careful not to step into that circle of light too suddenly: that if they moved into the light too suddenly, without thinking, they would perish in flame. Then, while I watched, one of them, the small, black man, moved into the light and crossed the bandstand and started fooling around with his drums. Then – being funny and being, also, extremely ceremonious –

Creole took Sonny by the arm and led him to the piano. A woman's voice called Sonny's name and a few hands started clapping. And Sonny, also being funny and being ceremonious, and so touched, I think, that he could have cried, but neither hiding it nor showing it, riding it like a man, grinned, and put both hands to his heart and bowed from the waist.

Creole then went to the bass fiddle and a lean, very bright-skinned brown man jumped up on the bandstand and picked up his horn. So there they were, and the atmosphere on the bandstand and in the room began to change and tighten. Someone stepped up to the microphone and announced them. Then there were all kinds of murmurs. Some people at the bar shushed others. The waitress ran around, frantically getting in the last orders, guys and chicks got closer to each other, and the lights on the bandstand, on the quartet, turned to a kind of indigo. Then they all looked different there. Creole looked about him for the last time, as though he were making certain that all his chickens were in the coop, and then he – jumped and struck the fiddle. And there they were.

All I know about music is that not many people ever really hear it. And even then, on the rare occasions when something opens within, and the music enters, what we mainly hear, or hear corroborated, are personal, private, vanishing evocations. But the man who creates the music is hearing something else, is dealing with the roar rising from the void and imposing order on it as it hits the air. What is evoked in him, then, is of another order, more terrible because it has no words, and triumphant, too, for that same reason. And his triumph, when he triumphs, is ours. I just watched Sonny's face. His face was troubled, he was working hard, but he wasn't with it. And I had the feeling that, in a way, everyone on the bandstand was waiting for him, both waiting for him and pushing him along. But as I began to watch Creole, I realized that it was Creole who held them all back. He had them on a short rein. Up there, keeping the beat with his whole body, wailing on the fiddle, with his eyes half closed, he was listening to everything, but he was listening to Sonny. He was having a dialogue with Sonny. He wanted Sonny to leave the shoreline and strike out for deep water. He was Sonny's witness that deep water and drowning were not the same thing – he had been there, and he knew. And he wanted Sonny to know. He was waiting for Sonny to do the things on the keys which would let Creole know that Sonny was in the water.

And, while Creole listened, Sonny moved, deep within, exactly like someone in torment. I had never before thought of how awful the relationship must be between the musician and his instrument. He has to fill it, this instrument, with the breath of life, his own. He has to make it do what he wants it to do. And a piano is just a piano. It's made out of so much wood and wires and little hammers and big ones, and ivory. While there's only so much you can do with it, the only way to find this out is to try; to try and make it do everything.

And Sonny hadn't been near a piano for over a year. And he wasn't on much better terms with his life, not the life that stretched before him now. He and the piano stammered, started one way, got scared, stopped; started another way, panicked, marked time, started again; then seemed to have found a direction, panicked again, got stuck. And the face I saw on Sonny I'd never seen before. Everything had been burned out of it, and, at the same time, things usually hidden were being burned in, by the fire and fury of the battle which was occurring in him up there.

Yet, watching Creole's face as they neared the end of the first set, I had the feeling that something had happened, something I hadn't heard. Then they finished, there was scattered applause, and then, without an instant's warning, Creole started into something else, it was almost sardonic, it was *Am I Blue*. And, as though he commanded, Sonny began to play. Something began to happen. And Creole let out the reins. The dry, low, black man said something awful on the drums, Creole answered, and the drums talked back. Then the horn insisted, sweet and high, slightly detached perhaps, and Creole listened, commenting now and then, dry, and driving, beautiful and calm and old. Then they all came together again, and

Sonny was part of the family again. I could tell this from his face. He seemed to have found, right there beneath his fingers, a damn brand-new piano. It seemed that he couldn't get over it. Then, for awhile, just being happy with Sonny, they seemed to be agreeing with him that brand-new pianos certainly were a gas.

Then Creole stepped forward to remind them that what they were playing was the blues. He hit something in all of them, he hit something in me, myself, and the music tightened and deepened, apprehension began to beat the air. Creole began to tell us what the blues were all about. They were not about anything very new. He and his boys up there were keeping it new, at the risk of ruin, destruction, madness, and death, in order to find new ways to make us listen. For, while the tale of how we suffer, and how we are delighted, and how we may triumph is never new, it always must be heard. There isn't any other tale to tell, it's the only light we've got in all this darkness.

And this tale, according to that face, that body, those strong hands on those strings, has another aspect in every country, and a new depth in every generation. Listen, Creole seemed to be saying, listen. Now these are Sonny's blues. He made the little black man on the drums know it, and the bright, brown man on the horn. Creole wasn't trying any longer to get Sonny in the water. He was wishing him Godspeed. Then he stepped back, very slowly, filling the air with the immense suggestion that Sonny speak for himself.

Then they all gathered around Sonny and Sonny played. Every now and again one of them seemed to say, amen. Sonny's fingers filled the air with life, his life. But that life contained so many others. And Sonny went all the way back, he really began with the spare, flat statement of the opening phrase of the song. Then he began to make it his. It was very beautiful because it wasn't hurried and it was no longer a lament. I seemed to hear with what burning he had made it his, with what burning we had yet to make it ours, how we could cease lamenting. Freedom lurked around us and I understood, at last, that he could help us to be free if we would listen, that he would never be free until we did. Yet, there was no battle in his face now. I heard what he had gone through, and would continue to go through until he came to rest in earth. He had made it his: that long line, of which we knew Mama and Daddy. And he was giving it back, as everything must be given back, so that, passing through death, it can live for ever. I saw my mother's face again, and felt, for the first time, how the stones of the road she had walked on must have bruised her feet. I saw the moonlit road where my father's brother died. And it brought something else back to me, and carried me past it, I saw my little girl again and felt Isabel's tears again, and I felt my own tears begin to rise. And I was yet aware that this was only a moment, that the world waited outside, as hungry as a tiger, and that trouble stretched above us, longer than the sky.

Then it was over. Creole and Sonny let out their breath, both soaking wet, and grinning. There was a lot of applause and some of it was real. In the dark, the girl came by and I asked her to take drinks to the bandstand. There was a long pause, while they talked up there in the indigo light and after a while I saw the girl put a Scotch and milk on top of the piano for Sonny. He didn't seem to notice it, but just before they started playing again, he sipped from it and looked towards me, and nodded. Then he put it back on top of the piano. For me, then, as they began to play again, it glowed and shook above my brother's head like the very cup of trembling.

The Rockpile

Across the street from their house, in an empty lot between two houses, stood the rockpile. It was a strange place to find a mass of natural rock jutting out of the ground; and someone, probably Aunt Florence, had once told them that the rock was there and could not be taken away because without it the subway cars underground would fly apart, killing all the people. This, touching on some natural mystery concerning the surface and the center of the earth, was far too intriguing an explanation to be challenged, and it invested the rockpile, moreover, with such mysterious importance that Roy felt it to be his right, not to say his duty, to play there.

Other boys were to be seen there each afternoon after school and all day Saturday and Sunday. They fought on the rockpile. Sure-footed, dangerous, and reckless, they rushed each other and grappled on the heights, sometimes disappearing down the other side in a confusion of dust and screams and upended, flying feet. 'It's a wonder they don't kill themselves,' their mother said, watching sometimes from the fire escape. 'You children stay away from there, you hear me?' Though she said 'children', she was looking at Roy, where he sat beside John on the fire escape. 'The good Lord knows,' she continued, 'I don't want you to come home bleeding like a hog every day the Lord sends.' Roy shifted impatiently, and continued to stare at the street, as though in this gazing he might somehow acquire wings. John said nothing. He had not really been spoken to: he was afraid of the rockpile and of the boys who played there.

Each Saturday morning John and Roy sat on the fire escape and watched the forbidden street below. Sometimes their mother sat in the room behind them, sewing, or dressing their younger sister, or nursing the baby, Paul. The sun fell across them and across the fire escape with a high, benevolent indifference; below them, men and women, and boys and girls, sinners all, loitered; sometimes one of the church-members passed and saw them and waved. Then, for the moment that they waved decorously back, they were intimidated. They watched the saint, man or woman, until he or she had disappeared from sight. The passage of one of the redeemed made them consider, however vacantly, the wickedness of the street, their own latent wickedness in sitting where they sat; and made them think of their father, who came home early on Saturdays and who would soon be turning this corner and entering the dark hall below them.

But until he came to end their freedom, they sat, watching and longing above the street. At the end of the street nearest their house was the bridge which spanned the Harlem River and led to a city called the Bronx; which was where Aunt Florence lived. Nevertheless, when they saw her coming, she did not come from the bridge, but from the opposite end of the street. This, weakly, to their minds, she explained by saying that she had taken the subway, not wishing to walk, and that, besides, she did not live in *that* section of the Bronx. Knowing that the Bronx was across the river, they did not believe this story ever, but, adopting towards her their father's attitude, assumed that she had just left some sinful place which she dared not name, as, for example, a movie palace.

In the summer-time boys swam in the river, diving off the wooden dock, or wading in from the garbage-heavy bank. Once a boy, whose name was Richard, drowned in the river. His mother had not known where he was: she had even come to their house, to ask if he was there. Then, in the evening, at six o'clock, they had heard from the street a woman screaming and wailing; and they ran to the windows and looked out. Down the street came the woman, Richard's mother, screaming, her face raised to the sky and tears running down her face. A woman walked beside her, trying to make her quiet and trying to hold her up. Behind them walked a man, Richard's father, with Richard's body in his arms. There were two white policemen walking in the gutter, who did not seem to know what should be done. Richard's father and Richard were wet, and Richard's body lay across his father's arms like a cotton baby. The woman's screaming filled all the street; cars slowed down and the people in the cars stared; people opened their windows and looked out and came rushing out of doors to stand in the gutter, watching. Then the small procession disappeared within the house which stood beside the rockpile. Then, '*Lord, Lord, Lord!*' cried Elizabeth, their mother, and slammed the window down.

On Saturday, an hour before his father would be coming home, Roy was wounded on the rockpile and brought screaming upstairs. He and John had been sitting on the fire escape and their mother had gone into the kitchen to sip tea with Sister McCandless. By and by Roy became bored and sat beside John in restless silence; and John began drawing into his schoolbook a newspaper advertisement which featured a new electric locomotive. Some friends of Roy passed beneath the fire escape and called him. Roy began to fidget, yelling down to them through the bars. Then a silence fell. John looked up. Roy stood looking at him.

'I'm going downstairs,' he said.

'You better stay where you is, boy. You know Mama don't want you going downstairs.'

'I be right *back*. She won't even know I'm gone, less you run and tell her.'

'I ain't *got* to tell her. What's going to stop her from coming in here and looking out the window?'

 'She's talking,' Roy said. He started into the house.

'But Daddy's going to be home soon!'

'I be back before *that*. What you all the time got to be so *scared* for?' He was already in the house and he now turned, leaning on the window sill, to swear impatiently. 'I be back in *five* minutes.'

John watched him sourly as he carefully unlocked the door and disappeared. In a moment he saw him on the sidewalk with his friends. He did not dare to go and tell his mother that Roy had left the fire escape because he had practically promised not to. He started to shout, *Remember, you said five minutes!* but one of Roy's friends was looking up at the fire escape. John looked down at his schoolbook: he became engrossed again in the problem of the locomotive.

When he looked up again he did not know how much time had passed, but now there was a gang fight on the rockpile. Dozens of boys fought each other in the harsh sun: clambering up the rocks and battling hand to hand, scuffed shoes sliding on the slippery rock; filling the bright air with curses and jubilant cries. They filled the air, too, with flying weapons: stones, sticks, tin cans, garbage, whatever could be picked up and thrown. John watched in a kind of absent amazement – until he remembered that Roy was still downstairs, and that he was one of the boys on the rockpile. Then he was afraid; he could not see his brother among the figures in the sun; and he stood up, leaning over the fire-escape railing. Then Roy appeared from the other side of the rocks; John saw that his shirt was torn; he was laughing. He moved until he stood at the very top of the rockpile. Then, something, an empty tin can, flew out of the air and hit him on the forehead, just above the eye. Immediately, one side of Roy's face ran with blood, he fell and rolled on his face down the rocks. Then for a moment there was no movement at all, no sound, the sun, arrested, lay on the street and the sidewalk and the arrested boys. Then someone screamed or shouted; boys began to run away, down the street, towards the bridge. The figure on the ground, having caught its breath and felt its own blood, began to shout. John cried, 'Mama! Mama!' and ran inside.

'Don't fret, don't fret,' panted Sister McCandless as they rushed down the dark, narrow, swaying stairs, 'don't fret. Ain't a boy been born don't get his knocks every now and again. *Lord!*' They hurried into the sun. A man had picked Roy up and now walked slowly towards them. One or two boys sat silent on their stoops; at either end of the street there was a group of boys watching. 'He ain't hurt bad,' the man said. 'Wouldn't be making this kind of noise if he was hurt real bad.'

Elizabeth, trembling, reached out to take Roy, but Sister McCandless, bigger, calmer, took him from the man and threw him over her shoulder as she once might have handled a sack of cotton. 'God bless you,' she said to the man, 'God bless you, son.' Roy was still screaming.

Elizabeth stood behind Sister McCandless to stare at his bloody face.

'It's just a flesh wound,' the man kept saying, 'just broke the skin, that's all.' They were moving across the sidewalk, towards the house. John, not now afraid of the staring boys, looked towards the corner to see if his father was yet in sight.

Upstairs, they hushed Roy's crying. They bathed the blood away, to find, just above the left eyebrow, the jagged, superficial scar. 'Lord, have mercy,' murmured Elizabeth, 'another inch and it would've been his eye.' And she looked with apprehension towards the clock. 'Ain't it the truth,' said Sister McCandless, busy with bandages and iodine.

'When did he go downstairs?' his mother asked at last.

Sister McCandless now sat fanning herself in the easy chair, at the head of the sofa where Roy lay, bound and silent. She paused for a moment to look sharply at John. John stood near the window, holding the newspaper advertisement and the drawing he had done.

'We was sitting on the fire escape,' he said. 'Some boys he knew called him.'

'When?'

'He said he'd be back in five minutes.'

'Why didn't you tell me he was downstairs?'

He looked at his hands, clasping his notebook, and did not answer.

'Boy,' said Sister McCandless, 'you hear your mother a-talking to you?'

He looked at his mother. He repeated:

'He said he'd be back in five minutes.'

'He said he'd be back in five minutes,' said Sister McCandless with scorn, 'don't look to me like that's no right answer. You's the man of the house, you supposed to look after your baby brothers and sisters – you ain't supposed to let them run off and get half killed. But I expect,' she added, rising from the chair, dropping the cardboard fan, 'your Daddy'll make you tell the truth. Your Ma's way too soft with you.'

He did not look at her, but at the fan where it lay in the dark red, depressed seat where she had been. The fan advertised a pomade for the hair and showed a brown woman and her baby, both with glistening hair, smiling happily at each other.

'Honey,' said Sister McCandless, 'I got to be moving along. Maybe I drop in later tonight. I don't reckon you going to be at Tarry Service tonight?'

Tarry Service was the prayer meeting held every Saturday night at church to strengthen believers and prepare the church for the coming of the Holy Ghost on Sunday.

'I don't reckon,' said Elizabeth. She stood up; she and Sister McCandless kissed each other on the cheek. 'But you be sure to remember me in your prayers.'

 'I surely will do that.' She paused, with her hand on

the door knob, and looked down at Roy and laughed. ‘Poor little man,’ she said, ‘reckon he’ll be content to sit on the fire escape *now*.’

Elizabeth laughed with her. ‘It sure ought to be a lesson to him. You don’t reckon,’ she asked nervously, still smiling, ‘he going to keep that scar, do you?’

‘Lord, no,’ said Sister McCandless, ‘ain’t nothing but a scratch. I declare, Sister Grimes, you worse than a child. Another couple of weeks and you won’t be able to *see* no scar. No, you go on about your housework, honey, and thank the Lord it weren’t no worse.’ She opened the door; they heard the sound of feet on the stairs. ‘I expect that’s the Reverend,’ said Sister McCandless, placidly. ‘I *bet* he going to raise Cain.’

‘Maybe it’s Florence,’ Elizabeth said. ‘Sometimes she get here about this time.’ They stood in the doorway, staring, while the steps reached the landing below and began again climbing to their floor. ‘No,’ said Elizabeth then, ‘that ain’t her walk. That’s Gabriel.’

‘Well, I’ll just go on,’ said Sister McCandless, ‘and kind of prepare his mind.’ She pressed Elizabeth’s hand as she spoke and started into the hall, leaving the door behind her slightly ajar. Elizabeth turned slowly back into the room. Roy did not open his eyes, or move; but she knew that he was not sleeping; he wished to delay until the last possible moment any contact with his father. John put his newspaper and his notebook on the table and stood, leaning on the table, staring at her.

'It wasn't my fault,' he said. 'I couldn't stop him from going downstairs.'

'No,' she said, 'you ain't got nothing to worry about. You just tell your Daddy the truth.'

He looked directly at her, and she turned to the window, staring into the street. What was Sister McCandless saying? Then from her bedroom she heard Delilah's thin wail and she turned, frowning, looking towards the bedroom and towards the still open door. She knew that John was watching her. Delilah continued to wail, she thought, angrily, *Now that girl's getting too big for that*, but she feared that Delilah would awaken Paul and she hurried into the bedroom. She tried to soothe Delilah back to sleep. Then she heard the front door open and close – too loud, Delilah raised her voice, with an exasperated sigh Elizabeth picked the child up. Her child and Gabriel's, her children and Gabriel's: Roy, Delilah, Paul. Only John was nameless and a stranger, living, unalterable testimony to his mother's days in sin.

'What happened?' Gabriel demanded. He stood enormous in the centre of the room, his black lunchbox dangling from his hand, staring at the sofa where Roy lay. John stood just before him, it seemed to her astonished vision just below him, beneath his fist, his heavy shoe. The child stared at the man in fascination and terror – when a girl down home she had seen rabbits stand so paralyzed before the barking dog. She hurried past Gabriel to the sofa, feeling the weight of Delilah in her arms like the weight of a shield, and stood over Roy, saying:

'Now, ain't a thing to get upset about, Gabriel. This boy sneaked downstairs while I had my back turned and got hisself hurt a little. He all right now.'

Roy, as though in confirmation, now opened his eyes and looked gravely at his father. Gabriel dropped his lunchbox with a clatter and knelt by the sofa.

'How you feel, son? Tell your Daddy what happened?'

Roy opened his mouth to speak and then, relapsing into panic, began to cry. His father held him by the shoulder.

'You don't want to cry. You's Daddy's little man. Tell your Daddy what happened.'

'He went downstairs,' said Elizabeth, 'where he didn't have no business to be, and got to fighting with them bad boys playing on that rockpile. That's what happened and it's a mercy it weren't nothing worse.'

He looked up at her. 'Can't you let this boy answer me for hisself?'

Ignoring this, she went on, more gently: 'He got cut on the forehead, but it ain't nothing to worry about.'

'You call a doctor? How you know it ain't nothing to worry about?'

'Is you got money to be throwing away on doctors? No, I ain't called no doctor. Ain't nothing wrong with my eyes that I can't tell whether he's hurt bad or not. He got a fright more'n anything else, and you ought to pray God it teaches him a lesson.'

'You got a lot to say *now*,' he said, 'but I'll have *me* something to say in a minute. I'll be wanting to know when all this happened, what you was doing with your eyes *then*.' He turned back to Roy, who had lain quietly sobbing, eyes wide open and body held rigid: and who now, at his father's touch, remembered the height, the sharp, sliding rock beneath his feet, the sun, the explosion of the sun, his plunge into darkness and his salty blood; and recoiled, beginning to scream, as his father touched his forehead. 'Hold still, hold still,' crooned his father, shaking, 'hold still. Don't cry. Daddy ain't going to hurt you, he just wants to see this bandage, see what they've done to his little man.' But Roy continued to scream and would not be still and Gabriel dared not lift the bandage for fear of hurting him more. And he looked at Elizabeth in fury: 'Can't you put that child down and help me with this boy? John, take your baby sister from your mother – don't look like neither of you got good sense.'

John took Delilah and sat down with her in the easy chair. His mother bent over Roy, and held him still, while his father, carefully – but still Roy screamed – lifted the bandage and stared at the wound. Roy's sobs began to lessen. Gabriel readjusted the bandage. 'You see,' said Elizabeth, finally, 'he ain't nowhere near dead.'

'It sure ain't your fault that he ain't dead.' He and Elizabeth considered each other for a moment in silence.

'He came mighty close to losing an eye. Course, his eyes ain't as big as your'n, so I reckon you don't think it matters so much.' At this her face hardened; he smiled. 'Lord, have mercy, he said, 'you think you ever going to learn to do right? Where was you when all this happened? Who let him go downstairs?'

'Ain't nobody let him go downstairs, he just went. He got a head just like his father, it got to be broken before it'll bow. I was in the kitchen.'

'Where was Johnnie?'

'He was in here.'

'Where?'

'He was on the fire escape.'

'Didn't he know Roy was downstairs?'

'I reckon.'

'What you mean, you reckon? He ain't got your big eyes for nothing, does he?' He looked over at John. 'Boy, you see your brother go downstairs?'

'Gabriel, ain't no sense in trying to blame Johnnie. You know right well if you have trouble making Roy behave, he ain't going to listen to his brother. He don't hardly listen to me.'

'How come you didn't tell your mother Roy was downstairs?'

John said nothing, staring at the blanket which covered Delilah.

'Boy, you hear me? You want me to take a strap to you?'

'No, you ain't,' she said. 'You ain't going to take no strap to this boy, not today you ain't. Ain't a soul to blame for Roy's lying up there now but you – you because you done spoiled him so that he thinks he can do just anything and get away with it. I'm here to tell you that ain't no way to raise no child. You don't pray to the Lord to help you do better than you been doing, you going to live to shed bitter tears that the Lord didn't take his soul today.' And she was trembling. She moved, unseeing, towards John and took Delilah from his arms. She looked back at Gabriel, who had risen, who stood near the sofa, staring at her. And she found in his face not fury alone, which would not have surprised her; but hatred so deep as to become insupportable in its lack of personality. His eyes were struck alive, unmoving, blind with malevolence – she felt, like the pull of the earth at her feet, his longing to witness her perdition. Again, as though it might be propitiation, she moved the child in her arms. And at this his eyes changed, he looked at Elizabeth, the mother of his children, the helpmeet given by the Lord. Then her eyes clouded; she moved to leave the room; her foot struck the lunchbox lying on the floor.

'John,' she said, 'pick up your father's lunchbox like a good boy.'

She heard, behind her, his scrambling movement as he left the easy chair, the scrape and jangle of the lunchbox as he picked it up, bending his dark head near the toe of his father's heavy shoe.

Previous Condition

I woke up shaking, alone in my room. I was clammy-cold with sweat, under me the sheet and the mattress were soaked. The sheet was grey and twisted like a rope. I breathed like I had been running.

I couldn't move for the longest while. I just lay on my back, spread-eagled, looking up at the ceiling, listening to the sounds of people getting up in other parts of the house, alarm clocks ringing and water splashing and doors opening and shutting and feet on the stairs. I could tell when people left for work: the hall door way downstairs whined and shuffled as it opened and gave a funny kind of double slam as it closed. One thud and then a louder thud and then a little final click. While the door was open I could hear the street sounds too, horses' hoofs and delivery wagons and people in the streets and big trucks and motor cars screaming on the asphalt.

I had been dreaming. At night I dreamt and woke up in the morning trembling, but not remembering the dream, except that in the dream I had been running. I could not remember when the dream – or dreams – had started; it had been long ago. For long periods maybe, I would have no dreams at all. And then they would come back, every night, I would try not to go to bed, I would go to sleep frightened and wake up frightened and have another day to get through with the nightmare at my shoulder. Now I was back from Chicago, busted, living off my friends in a dirty furnished room downtown. The show I had been with had folded in Chicago. It hadn't been much of a part – or much of a show either, to tell the truth. I played a kind of intellectual Uncle Tom, a young college student working for his race. The playwright had wanted to prove he was a liberal, I guess. But, as I say, the show had folded and here I was, back in New York and hating it. I knew that I should be getting another job, making the rounds, pounding the pavement. But I didn't. I couldn't face it. It was summer. I seemed to be fagged out. And every day I hated myself more. Acting's a rough life, even if you're white. I'm not tall and I'm not good looking and I can't sing or dance and I'm not white; so even at the best of times I wasn't in much demand.

The room I lived in was heavy ceilinged, perfectly square, with walls the colour of chipped dry blood. Jules Weissman, a Jewboy, had got the room for me. It's a room to sleep in, he said, or maybe to die in but God knows it wasn't meant to live in. Perhaps because the room was so hideous it had a fantastic array of light fixtures: one on the ceiling, one on the left wall, two on the right wall, and a lamp on the table beside my bed. My bed was in front of the window through which nothing ever blew but dust. It was a furnished room and they'd thrown enough stuff in it to furnish three rooms its size. Two easy chairs and a desk, the bed, the table, a straight-backed chair, a bookcase, a cardboard wardrobe; and my books and my suitcase, both unpacked; and my dirty clothes flung in a corner. It was the kind of room that defeated you. It had a fireplace, too, and a heavy marble mantelpiece and a great grey mirror above the mantelpiece. It was hard to see anything in the mirror very clearly – which was perhaps just as well – and it would have been worth your life to have started a fire in the fireplace.

'Well, you won't have to stay here long,' Jules told me the night I came. Jules smuggled me in, sort of, after dark, when everyone had gone to bed.

'Christ, I hope not.'

'I'll be moving to a big place soon,' Jules said. 'You can move in with me.' He turned all the lights on. 'Think it'll be all right for a while?' He sounded apologetic, as though he had designed the room himself.

'Oh, sure. D'you think I'll have any trouble?'

'I don't think so. The rent's paid. She can't put you out.'

I didn't say anything to that.

'Sort of stay undercover,' Jules said. 'You know.'

'Roger,' I said.

I had been living there for three days, timing it so I left

after everyone else had gone, coming back late at night when everyone else was asleep. But I knew it wouldn't work. A couple of the tenants had seen me on the stairs, a woman had surprised me coming out of the john. Every morning I waited for the landlady to come banging on the door. I didn't know what would happen. It might be all right. It might not be. But the waiting was getting me.

The sweat on my body was turning cold. Downstairs a radio was tuned in to the Breakfast Symphony. They were playing Beethoven. I sat up and lit a cigarette. 'Peter,' I said, 'don't let them scare you to death. You're a man, too.' I listened to Ludwig and I watched the smoke rise to the dirty ceiling. Under Ludwig's drums and horns I listened to hear footsteps on the stairs.

I'd done a lot of travelling in my time. I'd knocked about through St Louis, Frisco, Seattle, Detroit, New Orleans, worked at just about everything. I'd run away from my old lady when I was about sixteen. She'd never been able to handle me. You'll never be nothin' *but* a bum, she'd say. We lived in an old shack in a town in New Jersey in the nigger part of town, the kind of houses coloured people live in all over the US. I hated my mother for living there. I hated all the people in my neighborhood. They went to church and they got drunk. They were nice to the white people. When the landlord came around they paid him and took his crap.

The first time I was ever called nigger I was seven years old. It was a little white girl with long black curls. I used to leave the front of my house and go wandering by myself through town. This little girl was playing ball alone and as I passed her the ball rolled out of her hands into the gutter.

I threw it back to her.

'Let's play catch,' I said.

But she held the ball and made a face at me.

'My mother don't let me play with niggers,' she told me.

I did not know what the word meant. But my skin grew warm. I stuck my tongue out at her.

'I don't care. Keep your old ball.' I started down the street.

She screamed after me: 'Nigger, nigger, nigger!'

I screamed back: 'Your mother was a nigger!'

I asked my mother what a nigger was.

'Who called you that?'

'I heard somebody say it.'

'Who?'

'Just somebody.'

'Go wash your face,' she said. 'You dirty as sin. Your supper's on the table.'

I went to the bathroom and splashed water on my face and wiped my face and hands on the towel.

'You call that clean?' my mother cried. 'Come here, boy!'

She dragged me back to the bathroom and began to soap my face and neck.

'You run around dirty like you do all the time, everybody'll call you a little nigger, you hear?' She rinsed my face and looked at my hands and dried me. 'Now, go on and eat your supper.'

I didn't say anything. I went to the kitchen and sat down at the table. I remember I wanted to cry. My mother sat down across from me.

'Mama,' I said. She looked at me. I started to cry.

She came around to my side of the table and took me in her arms.

'Baby, don't fret. Next time somebody calls you nigger you tell them you'd rather be your color than be low-down and nasty like some white folks is.'

We formed gangs when I was older, my friends and I. We met white boys and their friends on the opposite sides of fences and we threw rocks and tin cans at each other.

I'd come home bleeding. My mother would slap me and scold me and cry.

'Boy, you wanna get killed? You wanna end up like your father?'

My father was a bum and I had never seen him. I was named for him: Peter.

I was always in trouble: truant officers, welfare workers, everybody else in town.

'You ain't never gonna be nothin' *but* a bum,' my mother said.

By and by older kids I knew finished school and got jobs and got married and settled down. They were going to settle down and bring more black babies into the world and pay the same rents for the same old shacks and it would go on and on –

When I was sixteen I ran away. I left a note and told Mama not to worry, I'd come back one day and I'd be all right. But when I was twenty-two she died. I came back and put my mother in the ground. Everything was like it had been. Our house had not been painted and the porch floor sagged and there was somebody's raincoat stuffed in the broken window. Another family was moving in.

Their furniture was stacked along the walls and their children were running through the house and laughing and somebody was frying pork chops in the kitchen. The oldest boy was tacking up a mirror.

Last year Ida took me driving in her big car and we passed through a couple of towns upstate. We passed some crumbling houses on the left. The clothes on the line were flying in the wind.

'Are people living there?' asked Ida.

'Just darkies,' I said.

Ida passed the car ahead, banging angrily on the horn. 'D'you know you're becoming paranoiac, Peter?'

'All right. All right. I know a lot of white people are starving too.'

'You're damn right they are. I know a little about poverty myself.'

Ida had come from the kind of family called shanty Irish. She was raised in Boston. She's a very beautiful woman who married young and married for money – so now I can afford to support attractive young men, she'd giggle. Her husband was a ballet dancer who was for ever on the road. Ida suspected that he went with boys. Not that I give a damn, she said, as long as he leaves me alone. When we met last year she was thirty and I was twenty-five. We had a pretty stormy relationship but we stuck. Whenever I got to town I called her; whenever I was stranded out of town I'd let her know. We never let it get too serious. She went her way and I went mine.

In all this running around I'd learned a few things. Like a prizefighter learns to take a blow or a dancer learns to fall, I'd learned how to get by. I'd learned never to be belligerent with policemen, for instance. No matter who was right, I was certain to be wrong. What might be accepted as just good old American independence in someone else would be insufferable arrogance in me. After the first few times I realized that I had to play smart, to act out the role I was expected to play. I only had one head and it was too easy to get it broken. When I faced a policeman I acted like I didn't know a thing. I let my jaw drop and I let my eyes get big. I didn't give him any smart answers, none of the crap about my rights. I figured out what answers he wanted and I gave them to him. I never let him think he wasn't king. If it was more than routine, if I was picked up on suspicion of robbery or murder in the neighborhood, I looked as humble as I could and kept my mouth shut and prayed. I took a couple of beatings but I stayed out of prison and I stayed off chain gangs. That was also due to luck, Ida pointed out once. 'Maybe it would've been better for you if you'd been a little less lucky. Worse things have happened than chain gangs. Some of them have happened to you.'

There was something in her voice. 'What are you talking about?' I asked.

'Don't lose your temper. I said maybe.'

'You mean you think I'm a coward?'

'I didn't say that, Peter.'

'But you meant that. Didn't you?'

'No. I didn't mean that. I didn't mean anything. Let's not fight.'

There are times and places when a Negro can use his color like a shield. He can trade on the subterranean Anglo-Saxon guilt and get what he wants that way; or some of what he wants. He can trade on his nuisance value, his value as forbidden fruit; he can use it like a knife, he can twist it and get his vengeance that way. I knew these things long before I realized that I knew them and in the beginning I used them, not knowing what I was doing. Then when I began to see it, I felt betrayed. I felt beaten as a person. I had no honest place to stand.

This was the year before I met Ida. I'd been acting in stock companies and little theatres; sometimes fairly good parts. People were nice to me. They told me I had talent. They said it sadly, as though they were thinking, What a pity, he'll never get anywhere. I had got to the point where I resented praise and I resented pity and I wondered what people were thinking when they shook my hand. In New York I met some pretty fine people; easy-going, hard-drinking, flotsam and jetsam; and they liked me; and I wondered if I trusted them; if I was able any longer to trust anybody. Not on top, where all the world could see, but underneath where everybody lives.

Soon I would have to get up. I listened to Ludwig. He shook the little room like the footsteps of a giant marching miles away. On summer evenings (and maybe we would go this summer) Jules and Ida and I would go up to the Stadium and sit beneath the pillars on the cold stone steps. There it seemed to me the sky was far away; and I was not myself, I was high and lifted up. We never talked, the three of us. We sat and watched the blue smoke curl in the air and watched the orange tips of cigarettes. Every once in a while the boys who sold popcorn and soda pop and ice cream climbed the steep steps chattering; and Ida shifted slightly and touched her blue-black hair; and Jules scowled. I sat with my knee up, watching the lighted half-moon below, the black-coated, straining conductor, the faceless men beneath him moving together in a rhythm like the sea. There were pauses in the music for the rushing, calling, halting piano. Everything would stop except the climbing soloist; he would reach a height and everything would join him, the violins first and then the horns; and then the deep blue bass and the flute and the bitter trampling drums; beating, beating and mounting together and stopping with a crash like daybreak. When I first heard the *Messiah* I was alone; my blood bubbled like fire and wine; I cried; like an infant crying for its mother's milk or a sinner running to meet Jesus.

Now below the music I heard footsteps on the stairs. I put out my cigarette. My heart was beating so hard I thought it would tear my chest apart. Someone knocked on the door.

I thought: Don't answer. Maybe she'll go away.

But the knocking came again, harder this time.

Just a minute, I said. I sat on the edge of the bed and put on my bathrobe. I was trembling like a fool. For Christ's sake, Peter, you've been through this before. What's the worst thing that can happen? You won't have a room. The world's full of rooms.

When I opened the door the landlady stood there, red-and-white-faced and hysterical.

'Who are you? I didn't rent this room to you.'

My mouth was dry. I started to say something.

'I can't have no colored people here,' she said. 'All my tenants are complainin'. Women afraid to come home nights.'

'They ain't gotta be afraid of me,' I said. I couldn't get my voice up; it rasped and rattled in my throat; and I began to be angry. I wanted to kill her. 'My friend rented this room for me,' I said.

'Well, I'm sorry, he didn't have no right to do that, I don't have nothin' against you, but you gotta get out.'

Her glasses blinked, opaque in the light on the landing. She was frightened to death. She was afraid of me but she was more afraid of losing her tenants. Her face was mottled with rage and fear, her breath came rushed and little bits of spittle gathered at the edges of her mouth; her breath smelled bad, like rotting hamburger on a July day.

'You can't put me out,' I said. 'This room was rented in my name.' I started to close the door, as though the matter was finished: 'I live here, see, this is my room, you can't put me out.'

'You get outa my house!' she screamed. 'I got the right to know who's in my house! This is a white neighborhood, I don't rent to colored people. Why don't you go on uptown, like you belong?'

'I can't stand niggers,' I told her. I started to close the door again but she moved and stuck her foot in the way. I wanted to kill her, I watched her stupid, wrinkled frightened white face and I wanted to take a club, hatchet, and bring it down with all my weight, splitting her skull down the middle where she parted her iron-grey hair.

'Get out of the door,' I said. 'I want to get dressed.'

But I knew that she had won, that I was already on my way. We stared at each other. Neither of us moved. From her came an emanation of fear and fury and something else. You maggot-eaten bitch, I thought. I said evilly, 'You wanna come in and watch me?' Her face didn't change, she didn't take her foot away. My skin prickled, tiny hot needles punctured my flesh. I was aware of my body under the bathrobe; and it was as though I had done something wrong, something monstrous, years ago, which no one had forgotten and for which I would be killed.

'If you don't get out,' she said, 'I'll get a policeman to put you out.'

I grabbed the door to keep from touching her. 'All right. All right. You can have the goddamn room. Now get out and let me dress.'

She turned away. I slammed the door. I heard her going down the stairs. I threw stuff into my suitcase. I tried to take as long as possible but I cut myself while shaving because I was afraid she would come back upstairs with a policeman.

Jules was making coffee when I walked in.

'Good morning, good morning! What happened to you?'

‘No room at the inn,’ I said. ‘Pour a cup of coffee for the notorious son of man.’ I sat down and dropped my suitcase on the floor.

Jules looked at me. ‘Oh. Well. Coffee coming up.’

He got out the coffee cups. I lit a cigarette and sat there. I couldn’t think of anything to say. I knew that Jules felt bad and I wanted to tell him that it wasn’t his fault.

He pushed coffee in front of me and sugar and cream.

‘Cheer up, baby. The world’s wide and life – life, she is very long.’

‘Shut up. I don’t want to hear any of your bad philosophy.’

‘Sorry.’

‘I mean, let’s not talk about the good, the true, and the beautiful.’

‘All right. But don’t sit there holding on to your table manners. Scream if you want to.’

‘Screaming won’t do any good. Besides I’m a big boy now.’

I stirred my coffee. ‘Did you give her a fight?’ Jules asked.

I shook my head. ‘No.’

‘Why the hell not?’

I shrugged; a little ashamed now. ‘I couldn’t have won it. What the hell.’

‘You might have won it. You might have given her a couple of bad moments.’

'Goddamit to hell, I'm sick of it. Can't I get a place to sleep without dragging it through the courts? I'm goddamn tired of battling every Tom, Dick, and Harry for what everybody else takes for granted. I'm tired! Have you ever been sick to death of something? Well, I'm sick to death. And I'm scared. I've been fighting so goddamn long I'm not a person any more. I'm not Booker T. Washington. I've got no vision of emancipating anybody. I want to emancipate myself. If this goes on much longer, they'll send me to Bellevue, I'll blow my top, I'll break somebody's head. I'm not worried about that miserable little room. I'm worried about what's happening to me, *to me*, inside. I don't walk the streets, I crawl. I've never been like this before. Now when I go to a strange place I wonder what will happen, will I be accepted, if I'm accepted, can I accept? –'

'Take it easy,' Jules said.

'Jules, I'm beaten.'

'I don't think you are. Drink your coffee.'

'Oh,' I cried, 'I know you think I'm making it dramatic, that I'm paranoiac and just inventing trouble! Maybe I think so sometimes, how can I tell? You get so used to being hit you find you're always waiting for it. Oh, I know, you're Jewish, you get kicked around, too, but you can walk into a bar and nobody *knows* you're Jewish and if you go looking for a job you'll get a better job than mine! How can I say what it feels like? I don't know. I know everybody's in trouble and nothing is easy, but how can I explain to you what it feels like to be black when I don't understand it and don't want to and spend all my time trying to forget it? I don't want to hate anybody – but now maybe, I can't love anybody either – are we friends? Can we be really friends?'

'We're friends,' Jules said, 'don't worry about it.' He scowled. 'If I wasn't Jewish I'd ask you why you don't live in Harlem.' I looked at him. He raised his hand and smiled – 'But I'm Jewish, so I didn't ask you. Ah, Peter,' he said, 'I can't help you – take a walk, get drunk, we're all in this together.'

I stood up. 'I'll be around later. I'm sorry.'

'Don't be sorry. I'll leave my door open. Bunk here for awhile.'

'Thanks,' I said.

I felt that I was drowning; that hatred had corrupted me like cancer in the bone.

I saw Ida for dinner. We met in a restaurant in the Village, an Italian place in a gloomy cellar with candles on the tables.

It was not a busy night, for which I was grateful. When I came in there were only two other couples on the other side of the room. No one looked at me. I sat down in a corner booth and ordered a Scotch old-fashioned. Ida was late and I had three of them before she came.

She was very fine in black, a high-necked dress with a pearl choker; and her hair was combed page-boy style, falling just below her ears.

'You look real sweet, baby.'

'Thank you. It took fifteen extra minutes but I hoped it would be worth it.'

'It was worth it. What're you drinking?'

'Oh – what're you drinking?'

'Old-fashioneds.'

She sniffed and looked at me. 'How many?'

I laughed. 'Three.'

'Well,' she said, 'I suppose you had to do something.' The waiter came over. We decided on one Manhattan and one lasagna and one spaghetti with clam sauce and another old-fashioned for me.

'Did you have a constructive day, sweetheart? Find a job?'

'Not today,' I said. I lit her cigarette. 'Metro offered me a fortune to come to the coast and do the lead in *Native Son* but I turned it down. Type casting, you know. It's so difficult to find a decent part.'

'Well, if they don't come up with a decent offer soon tell them you'll go back to Selznick. *He'll* find you a part with guts – the very *idea* of offering you *Native Son*! I wouldn't stand for it.'

'You ain't gotta tell me. I told them if they didn't find me a decent script in two weeks I was through, that's all.'

'Now that's talking, Peter my lad.'

The drinks came and we sat in silence for a minute or two. I finished half of my drink at a swallow and played with the toothpicks on the table. I felt Ida watching me.

'Peter, you're going to be awfully drunk.'

'Honeychile, the first thing a southern gentleman learns is how to hold his liquor.'

'That myth is older than the rock of ages. And anyway you come from Jersey.'

I finished my drink and snarled at her: 'That's just as good as the South.'

Across the table from me I could see that she was readying herself for trouble: her mouth tightened slightly, setting her chin so that the faint cleft showed: 'What happened to you today?'

I resented her concern; I resented my need. 'Nothing worth talking about,' I muttered, 'just a mood.'

And I tried to smile at her, to wipe away the bitterness.

'Now I know something's the matter. Please tell me.'

It sounded trivial as hell: 'You know the room Jules found for me? Well, the landlady kicked me out of it today.'

'God save the American republic,' Ida said. 'D'you want to waste some of my husband's money? We can sue her.'

'Forget it. I'll end up with lawsuits in every state in the union.'

'Still, as a gesture –'

'The devil with the gesture. I'll get by.'

The food came. I didn't want to eat. The first mouthful hit my belly like a gong. Ida began cutting up lasagna.

'Peter,' she said, 'try not to feel so badly. We're all in this together, the whole world. Don't let it throw you. What can't be helped you have to learn to live with.'

'That's easy for you to say,' I told her.

She looked at me quickly and looked away. 'I'm not pretending that it's easy to do,' she said.

I didn't believe that she could really understand it; and there was nothing I could say. I sat like a child being scolded, looking down at my plate, not eating, not saying anything. I wanted her to stop talking, to stop being intelligent about it, to stop being calm and grown-up about it; good Lord, none of us has ever grown up, we never will.

'It's no better anywhere else,' she was saying. 'In all of Europe there's famine and disease, in France and England they hate the Jews – nothing's going to change, baby, people are too empty-headed, too empty-hearted – it's always been like that, people always try to destroy what they don't understand – and they hate almost everything because they understand so little –'

I began to sweat in my side of the booth. I wanted to stop her voice. I wanted her to eat and be quiet and leave me alone. I looked around for the waiter so I could order another drink. But he was on the far side of the restaurant, waiting on some people who had just come in; a lot of people had come in since we had been sitting there.

'Peter,' Ida said, 'Peter please don't look like that.'

I grinned: the painted grin of the professional clown. 'Don't worry, baby, I'm all right. I know what I'm going to do. I'm gonna go back to my people where I belong and find me a nice, black nigger wench and raise me a flock of babies.'

Ida had an old maternal trick; the grin tricked her into using it now. She raised her fork and rapped me with it across the knuckles. 'Now, stop that. You're too old for that.'

I screamed and stood up screaming and knocked the candle over: 'Don't *do* that, you bitch, don't *ever* do that!'

She grabbed the candle and set it up and glared at me. Her face had turned perfectly white: 'Sit down! Sit *down*!'

I fell back into my seat. My stomach felt like water. Everyone was looking at us. I turned cold, seeing what they were seeing: a black boy and a white woman, alone together. I knew it would take nothing to have them at my throat.

'I'm sorry,' I muttered, 'I'm sorry, I'm sorry.'

The waiter was at my elbow. 'Is everything all right, miss?'

'Yes, quite, thank you.' She sounded like a princess

dismissing a slave. I didn't look up. The shadow of the waiter moved away from me.

'Baby,' Ida said, 'forgive me, please forgive me.'

I stared at the tablecloth. She put her hand on mine, brightness and blackness.

'Let's go,' I said, 'I'm terribly sorry.'

She motioned for the check. When it came she handed the waiter a ten-dollar bill without looking. She picked up her bag.

'Shall we go to a night-club or a movie or something?'

'No, honey, not tonight.' I looked at her. 'I'm tired, I think I'll go on over to Jules's place. I'm gonna sleep on his floor for a while. Don't worry about me. I'm all right.'

She looked at me steadily. She said: 'I'll come see you tomorrow?'

'Yes, baby, please.'

The waiter brought the change and she tipped him. We stood up; as we passed the tables (not looking at the people) the ground under me seemed falling, the doorway seemed impossibly far away. All my muscles tensed; I seemed ready to spring; I was waiting for the blow.

I put my hands in my pockets and we walked to the end of the block. The lights were green and red, the lights from the theatre across the street exploded blue and yellow, off and on.

'Peter?'

'Yes?'

'I'll see you tomorrow?'

'Yeah. Come by Jules's. I'll wait for you.'

'Good night, darling.'

'Good night.'

I started to walk away. I felt her eyes on my back. I kicked a bottle-top on the sidewalk.

God save the American republic.

I dropped into the subway and got on an uptown train, not knowing where it was going and not caring. Anonymous, islanded people surrounded me, behind newspapers, behind make-up, fat, fleshy masks and flat eyes. I watched the empty faces. (No one looked at me.) I looked at the ads, unreal women and pink-cheeked men selling cigarettes, candy, shaving cream, night gowns, chewing gum, movies, sex; sex without organs, drier than sand and more secret than death. The train stopped. A white boy and a white girl got on. She was nice, short, svelte. Nice legs. She was hanging on his arm. He was the football type, blond, ruddy. They were dressed in summer clothes. The wind from the doors blew her print dress. She squealed, holding the dress at the knees and giggled and looked at him. He said something I didn't catch and she looked at me and the smile died. She stood so that she faced him and had her back to me. I looked back at the ads. Then I hated them. I wanted to do something to make them hurt, something that would crack the pink-cheeked mask. The white boy and I did not look at each other again. They got off at the next stop.

I wanted to keep on drinking. I got off in Harlem and went to a run-down bar on Seventh Avenue. My people, my people. Sharpies stood on the corner, waiting. Women in summer dresses pranced by on wavering heels. Click clack. Click clack. There were white mounted policemen in the streets. On every block there was another policeman on foot. I saw a black cop.

God save the American republic.

The juke box was letting loose with 'Hamp's Boogie'. The place was jumping, I walked over to the man.

'Rye,' I said.

I was standing next to somebody's grandmother. 'Hello, papa. What you puttin' down?'

'Baby, you can't pick it up,' I told her. My rye came and I drank.

'Nigger,' she said, 'you must think you's somebody.'

I didn't answer. She turned away, back to her beer, keeping time to the juke box, her face sullen and heavy and aggrieved. I watched her out of the side of my eye. She had been good-looking once, pretty even, before she hit the bottle and started crawling into too many beds. She was flabby now, flesh heaved all over in her thin dress. I wondered what she'd be like in bed; then I realized that I was a little excited by her; I laughed and set my glass down.

'The same,' I said. 'And a beer chaser.'

The juke box was playing something else now, something brassy and commercial which I didn't like. I kept on drinking, listening to the voices of my people, watching the faces of my people. (God pity us, the terrified republic.) Now I was sorry to have angered the woman who still sat next to me, now deep in conversation with another, younger woman. I longed for some opening, some sign, something to make me part of the life around me. But there was nothing except my color. A white outsider coming in would have seen a young Negro drinking in a Negro bar, perfectly in his element, in his place, as the saying goes. But the people here knew differently, as I did. I didn't seem to have a place.

So I kept on drinking by myself, saying to myself after each drink, Now I'll go. But I was afraid; I didn't want to sleep on Jules's floor; I didn't want to go to sleep. I kept on drinking and listening to the juke box. They were playing Ella Fitzgerald, 'Cow-Cow Boogie'.

'Let me buy you a drink,' I said to the woman.

She looked at me, startled, suspicious, ready to blow her top.

'On the level,' I said. I tried to smile. 'Both of you.'

'I'll take a beer,' the young one said.

I was shaking like a baby. I finished my drink.

'Fine,' I said. I turned to the bar.

'Baby,' said the old one, 'what's your story?'

The man put three beers on the counter.

'I got no story, Ma,' I said.

READ MORE IN PENGUIN